ALIENS

Look out for the other exciting titles by
Colin & Jacqui Hawkins in the same series:

**Monsters • Witches • Spooks •
Vampires • Pirates • School**

First published in hardback in Great Britain
by HarperCollins Publishers Ltd in 1996
First published in Picture Lions in 1997
10 9 8 7 6 5 4 3 2 1
ISBN: 0 00 664619 0
Picture Lions is an imprint of the Children's
Division, part of HarperCollins Publishers Ltd,
77-85 Fulham Palace Road, Hammersmith,
London W6 8JB.
Text and illustrations copyright
© Colin and Jacqui Hawkins 1996
The author and illustrator assert the moral
right to be identified as the author and
illustrator of the work.
A CIP catalogue for this title is available from
the British Library.
Printed and bound in Hong Kong.

ALIENS

COLIN AND JACQUI HAWKINS

PictureLions

An Imprint of HarperCollinsPublishers

TAKE ME TO YOUR LEADER!

Imagine this: you are travelling in a car very late at night. The road is dark and lonely... you are miles from anywhere. Suddenly a gigantic dark shape rumbles out of the night sky. The ground shakes and trembles, the air vibrates... a blinding white light hits the car. Try not to be afraid, there is nowhere to hide. You cannot escape, you are about to meet...

Creatures who are not of this world, creatures who have travelled from the farthest reaches of the Galaxy and beyond. Glowing and gruesome, green and globby, squirming and tentacled, ghastly, grey and grim.

THEY ARE THE...

Aliens!

SNOITATULAS

Why Do Aliens Visit Earth?

Do they come in peace or are their intentions hostile? Have they come to destroy the Earth and enslave humankind? Or are they just here on a package holiday to see Disneyland, the Tower of London and get an all-over suntan? Perhaps they want to make contact and befriend humans in order to teach us the secrets of the Universe, or perhaps they are here to warn us...

Within the pages of this book you may find some of the answers to these questions, or you may not. But you will learn of some extraordinary extraterrestrial experiences.

Read on... May the force be with you.

ALIEN SPOTTER'S GUIDE, PART 1

Aliens come in many different shapes, sizes and colours. Here are a few of the more popular types. Have you spotted any of these?

Peace Man.

Little Green Men

Professor Johannis thought he was seeing double when he was followed up a mountain in Italy by these little dwarf-like aliens. They had green heads, popping eyes, fishy mouths and very bad breath. Professor Johannis does not want to repeat the experience.

SILLY SPACE:
ALIEN TEACHER: What is an atom?
ALIEN PUPIL: The earthling who lived with Eve in the Garden of Eden.

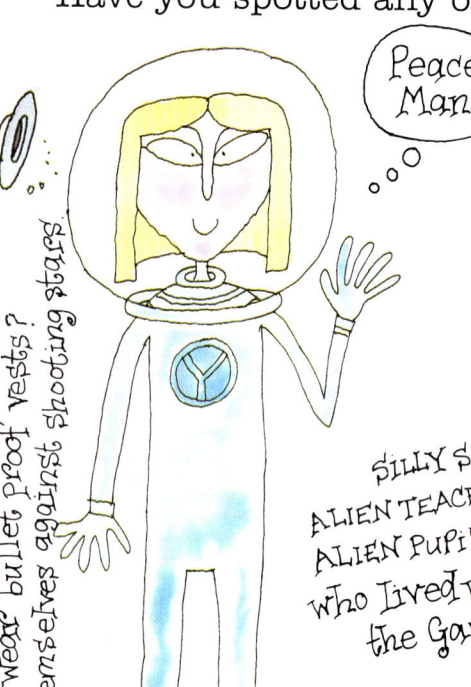

Why do aliens wear bullet proof vests? To protect themselves against shooting stars.

The Greys

These are little aggressive aliens with big heads, large black eyes and no sense of humour who use a 'mind-wipe'* technique. They are responsible for most abductions and there are numerous reportings of their presence on Earth.

We are not amused

Nordic

A very common type of alien, they are friendly and peace-loving with long blonde hair and are fond of wearing ski-suits. They communicate telepathically as they did with George Adamski* in the 1950s.

* George Adamski was a famous abductee who lived in America in the 50s and had frequent contact with aliens.

* Have you ever experienced memory loss, especially in school - this might mean you've been abducted. Tell this to your teacher when you forget your homework.

Speak to an alien. From long distance.

Hairy Dwarfs

These very small, hairy aliens are very fond of wearing fur coats. They have also been seen wearing helmets – perhaps our air is too polluted for them.

Goblin

This goblin-like alien was spotted in Kentucky, USA in 1955. It was about 1.2 metres tall, was able to float and reports were that it had a most macabre sense of humour. Although it was shot at several times, gunfire had absolutely no effect.

Tin Man of Japan

Be careful of these robotic aliens as you can get right up their noses, as happened to unfortunate Mr Amano of Japan*. If you should be unlucky enough to meet one of these aliens, it will press its metallic pipe-like nose against your head in an effort to communicate. This could give you a headache.

Ed's Note: Read about Mr Amano later in 'They Came From Outer Space'

I nose you.

Mushroom Head

This alien was seen by David Stephens of USA in 1955. He was abducted by Mushroom Head and then medically examined on board his ship. The alien communicated telepathically and seemed friendly, but very secretive. It was declared that the spaceship was very small and there wasn't mushroom.

Tell no one that you have seen me

Grey Ghost

These pale, ghost-like aliens are about 1.5 metres tall, with grey, wrinkled skin, and crab-like claws or pincers. In 1973 Charles Higson and Calvin Parker of Mississippi, USA met these strange creatures who made a buzzing noise as they floated towards them. "It was time to buzz off," said the friends, "so we did."

I moth go now.

Mothman Mystery

Lothian Council in Scotland put up a plaque marking an alien encounter with 'Mothman' in 1992. Yet, nine months later, the plaque mysteriously went missing. Could it have been abducted by aliens?

Mothman

A bizarre type of alien covered in hair with a huge wingspan, it seems to be a cross between a man and a moth (hence its name) with huge, shining, red eyes. There have been numerous sightings around the world and, at the time of these sightings, many people discovered enormous holes in their clothes! Roger Scarberry and Steve Mallette in 1966 in Virginia, USA reported that 'Mothman' had swept towards their car and chased them for many miles. Perhaps it was attracted to the car's headlights like a moth!

Deep-Sea Diver

This type of alien was seen by a young boy, Henry Thomson, in Lancashire, England in 1926. It seemed to be wearing a thickly-padded, silver-grey suit like a diver. Last seen heading for the local chippie.

Why do aliens carry umbrellas? Because umbrellas can't walk.

'Scale-Suit' Alien

This alien was seen in Argentina in 1968. It was 1.8 metres tall, dressed in a shiny blue suit covered in scales (perhaps an alien shell-suit?) and it spoke in a strange language which sounded like Chinese. Hovering above the alien's left hand was a glowing sphere.

The Men in Black (MIBs)

These cold, sinister individuals are dressed all in black, with red, glowing eyes. They look like hoodlums from a 50s B movie, or possibly members of the Mafia or even Secret Service men. They are telepathic, very secretive and extremely frightening. Often seen driving large black limos with blacked-out windows. The car number plates are always unregistered when checked by alien spotters.

Many ufologists* have been visited by these menacing aliens and told to keep their mouths shut about their experiences... or else.

Ed's Note: People who study UFOs and track their movements.

Very Anteresting

It's a scientific theory that aliens could be a species of insect as their bodies are very well adapted to withstand the pressures of space travel at hyper-light* speed as they beetle about space.

Ed's Note: over and above the speed of light, in other words, very fast!

UNIDENTIFIED FLYING OBJECTS, PART 1

UFOs are usually metallic and smooth. They fly noiselessly and sometimes appear to change colour and glow bright red as they accelerate. Many different shapes have been sighted and recorded.

Here are a few of them.

UFO FACT Many sightings in different countries are made by policemen. Are aliens obsessed by uniforms?

Don't worry boys, there's sure to be a rational explanation.

Ging Gang Goolie?

In 1957, Scout Master, C. Desverges, stopped his van to investigate a bright light in the bushes. He saw a UFO which hovered above him, a ball of red mist emerged from the UFO and engulfed him. It burned his hat, singed his hair and made his woggle warm. The scouts ran off... to get help.

In Over Their Heads

Just before dawn in Ohio, USA in 1966 two policeman had a very close encounter with a UFO flying low over them. It hovered overhead, humming loudly and was so bright it gave them a headache. The UFO moved off at great speed and got a good head start but the policeman headed after it. Seventy kms along the road they came head to head with another cop observing the UFO. They were very relieved that the other cop had also witnessed the alien craft and that they were not completely off their heads.

What d'ya reckon that is, Orville?

I reckon that's a giant ceegar shaped flying object.

Lighting Up the Sky

In Wisconsin, USA in the 1980s several policemen saw a cigar-shaped UFO. "This is a no smoking zone," said the local sheriff. "It just shouldn't be here!"

Great Balls of Fire!

In 1952 a group of friends were chased by a monstrous alien which emerged from a glowing throbbing UFO.

EEK!

Mad Cows in Texas

In 1957 some cowboys and their steers saw a sausage-shaped UFO shoot across the sky at an estimated speed of 1500 kms an hour.
Was it on steeroids?

I am, I am.

Must be doing 1500 kms an hour

Will ya look at that?

RECOMMENDED READING FOR ALIENS:
'Lost in Space' by I. Malone.
'How To Shoot Aliens' by Ray Gunn.
'Never Make A Girl Alien Angry.' by Sheila Tack.

Eggstraordinary!

Brazilian farmer, Antonio Villas Boas, claimed that an egg-shaped UFO landed in his field causing his tractor to break down. Boas had many contacts with aliens throughout his life* – once even claiming that he had been eggstensively eggsamined!

* Ed's Note: More about him later.

OLD ALIEN JOKE: What did the alien say when he landed in a field of weeds?
Take me to your weeder.

What's That, Uncle? In 1971 a farm manager and his nephew were working on a ranch in Argentina where they saw a glowing alien spacecraft with long antennae protruding from it. After hovering over them for some time, it then sped off.

UFOs = unidentified flying objects

Sightings of UFOs have been reported from every corner of the earth. As a hobby, Ufology* is simply out of this world.

Have you ever thought about becoming a Ufologist?

*Ed's Note: The study of UFOs

Turnip the heat, it's freezing in here

There was a young alien named Bright,
Who travelled much faster than light,
He started one day, in a relative way,
And returned on the previous night.

A Turnip for the Books
An alien spaceship which looked like a giant turnip landed in a field near Caracas, Venezuela, South America.

GREETINGS EARTHLING.

Och! I canna believe it! ... a UFO!

Aliens from outer space are star craving mad.

Monstrous Sighting
In 1971, a UFO looking like a steam iron was sighted near Loch Ness in Scotland. The local inhabitants got very steamed up about the incident. "It could frighten Nessie, the wee beestie."

Jetting Jelly

In Minnesota, USA in October 1965, a glowing jelly-like flying saucer wobbled across the sky at great speed. It was booked for speeding by a local policeman but it just whirred off. Its present whirrabouts are now unknown.

E HORROR ON LE HIGHWAY

)ne August night in 1975, Monsieur Cyrus, a retired policeman, was driving home in South West France when suddenly he encountered a UFO on the road and slammed on his brakes. As the machine hovered in the air above him, he was blinded by the fierce light projected from the underside of the ship and his car shook and vibrated violently.

"Oui, it was 'orrible and 'orrific," said a shaken Monsieur Cyrus in an alien voice.

SupaSnaps

A photograph of a UFO taken by a farmer in Oregon, USA is considered to be genuine by experts. The farmer has spare prints if the aliens would like to contact him.

What The UFO!

Is Anyone There?

Many astronauts have reported UFOs. Astronaut James Young said that, "there are so many stars that it is mathematically improbable that there aren't life sources in the Universe." What do you think?

What do you call a mad spaceman? An astronut.

SPACED OUT HUMOUR
What do you call an alien's watch?
A lunar tick.

Gotcha.

Good shooting Zork

Star Wars

When the spacecraft Phobos II was orbiting Mars on March 29 1989, Soviet Mission Control lost contact with the craft in mysterious circumstances. It is possible the Soviet spaceship was attacked by an alien craft – the last pictures sent back to earth revealed a dark saucer shape hovering between Phobos II and the planet surface. Was this the beginning of Star Wars?

Space crew on Apollo 11 and Apollo 12 both reported UFOs.

WHY FLYING SAUCERS?
In space there is no gravity, no wind resistance, no up or down. It is therefore thought that the most efficient shape to travel through space is the flying saucer.

What's that Ed?

It could be life Jim, but not as we know it.

By Gemini

Astronauts Ed White and James McDivitt on spacecraft Gemini II in June 1965 saw a UFO with several long arms sticking out of it. As it was armed, the astronauts kept their distance.

Kenneth Arnold was the first person to use the term 'flying saucer'. In 1947 he was flying near Washington when he saw nine flying saucers flying in formation.*

* An early ufologist's tongue-twister.

Over... And Out...

Australian pilot, Frederick Valentich, took off from Melbourne Airport in October 1978 and was never seen again. His last reported radio transmission recorded the very close proximity of a UFO and his final message was, "It's right above me now... and coming down closer..."
The radio operators then heard a scraping, metallic noise... and then there was silence...

SPACE SNIGGER
What do you call an alien with a sausage on his head?
A head-banger.

Mon dieu.

Sacre bleu.

Ooo Ooo Boo (Bonjour Frenchie)

Boo oo Og! (Watch out he has a baguette)

Le Pain!*

French steel-worker Marius DeWilde was alerted by his dog howling. He discovered two very weird creatures near a spacecraft. They were very short, about one metre tall, dressed in spacesuits with large helmets. They also were very ugly, with broad shoulders but no arms. "The spacecraft shot a beam that paralysed me," said Marius, "so they weren't completely 'armless aliens." * joke for linguists.

Strange But True

Many people believe that the strange objects that fall from our skies are from UFOs. Aliens are also thought to be responsible for collecting people and samples from earth to examine and study.

Hi.

Nice of you to drop in.

Sky Diver's Shock

A sky diver in America jumped out of an aeroplane and totally disappeared. When she was found three days later she claimed that she had been intercepted by aliens on her free-fall descent. A lot of people thought she was making it up but as her parachute had not been opened, how on earth did she arrive back on Earth?

TASTY TICKLER — What is pink and soft and comes from space? A Martian mallow.

Jellies from Heaven

Slimy globs as large as a fist fell out of the sky on to the basketball court of Upper Lake High School. The science teacher thought they were 'some kind of egg and might hatch out'. A curious student tasted one and said it tasted salty – but he preferred crisps.

GEE!

I love jelly babies

In a Spin

Park Ranger, Paul Perryman and his horse were startled one day in 1990 when a blue, cone-shaped spinner fell from the sky near them. It was discovered that the spinner had fallen from the propeller hub of an aeroplane propeller but that no planes had lost this part recently. Weirdest of all was that the spinner was thought to date from World War II.

WEIRD!

- A turtle encased in ice fell from the sky.
- An alligator was dropped on Charleston, USA.
- Thousands of snakes fell in Memphis, USA.
- In Birmingham, England, tiny frogs fell during a thunderstorm.
- During a storm in Russia, hundreds of silver coins fell out of the sky.

This is a photo of a UFO. But don't tell anyone it was me that showed it to you. OK.

How do you arrange a trip to Mars to visit aliens? You planet.

Caught on Camera

On 2 April 1965, a UFO was seen flying at a height of 50 metres above Melbourne, Australia. The man who photographed it wishes to remain anonymous. (His photograph is regarded by experts as genuine.)

SPACE SPOOF
hy are aliens so forgetful? cause everything ou tell them es in one ear d out of the others!

UFO FACT
In many UFO sightings, a strange substance called 'angel hair' has fallen from the sky. It is a white silky thread-like substance like a spider's web.

Heavy Metal

In 1947, a large chunk of metal allegedly dropped from a UFO. Mr Dahl of Washington was in his boat when metal rained down from a huge flying saucer. Some of the metal smashed through the wheelhouse of his boat.

Star Jelly

In 1883 in New Jersey, USA, star jelly fell out of the sky like a fiery rain. A milkmaid and her cow were startled when the slimy substance fell all around them from whey up in the sky.

This is mysteerious

SPACE FACT
40 million UFO sightings reported since 1947.

EXTRAORDINARY EXTRATERRESTRIAL EXPERIENCES!

I think you'll have to grill and bear it

What do you think Doc?

LOONY LAUGHTER
What do you call an alien with 30 eyes, 10 ears, 4 noses and 3 mouths?
— Sir.

Too Hot to Handle!

Unfortunate Stephen Michalak was sitting on the edge of Lake Falcon in Manitoba, Canada, when a UFO landed near him. When he went up and touched it, the heat melted his glove. Then as the UFO took off into the sky, the hot exhaust fumes hit Michalak on his chest and set his clothes on fire. He managed to put out the fire but was scarred and charred by the experience. UFO researchers were faced with a burning question. Did Michalak really see a UFO or was he suffering from an over-heated imagination?

ALIEN: I didn't come to Earth to be insulted.
EARTHLING: No — where do you usually go?

Hey, Chuck where ya going?

I know...Miss...
I know Miss...
I know everything
Miss... I know...
Miss...

Bright Spark?

Do Extraterrestrial Experiences make you more intelligent? Would you like to be a Space Ace? Welsh schoolgirl, Gaynor Sunderland, became super bright after an encounter with a UFO in July 1978. Do you know any kids like this? Perhaps they have been in touch with aliens.

Perhaps they are aliens?

What ya doing Chuck?

A Fishy Story!

In August 1976, four friends set off for a canoe trip in Maine, USA. But the fun-filled adventure rapidly turned into a night of horror when rumbling towards them came a large UFO. As the men started paddling desperately to shore, a beam of light shot down from the spacecraft straight at them. The men thought that they would never escape. Suddenly they found themselves on shore. Feeling dazed and confused, they were shocked to find their huge camp-fire completely burnt to embers. Where had all the time gone? Under hypnosis, the friends all told the same remarkable story that the beam of light had caught and drawn them up into an alien spacecraft where they were medically examined by aliens and then returned to the shore unhurt. Perhaps the aliens thought their catch too tiddly? Who knows.

What would you say if aliens invited you to their spaceship? – Thank them for the invitation but say you have to go home for tea.
– Say that you have been told never to go with strangers.
– Tell them you've too much homework to do.

Alien Abductions

Have you ever been abducted?

Signs to look out for:
- pyjamas on inside out
- strange puncture marks on skin
- missing time and loss of memory
- dirty hands and feet

Barking Mad

Antonio Villas Boas* from Brazil claimed he had been abducted by small aliens wearing space suits and helmets. They took him inside their spaceship where he met an alien woman who took blood from his chin and barked at him – WOOF! WOOF!

* Ed's Note: See UFOs, Part 1

Shooting Star

In 1974, Carl Higson of Wyoming, USA was out hunting in the forest. He had just shot at some elks when a humanoid* appeared called 'Ausso'. Ausso was a bow-legged, chinless wonder, with only a few teeth, spiky hair and strange implements instead of hands.

Ausso gave Higson a capsule which he swallowed and then found himself inside a transparent cubicle – with Ausso and the elks.

They were all hurtled into space to a dark star where Higson was given a medical examination by the aliens before being returned to earth.

* Ed's Note: a humanoid is something resembling a human form. Do you look like Ausso or do you know anyone who does?

How Sickening

Leo Childers became sick when he was abducted in a spaceship so the aliens held him out of the window. At the time the ship was allegedly travelling at 400,000 kms per hour!

How Unfortunate!

Fortunato Zanfretta was captured and abducted by hairy aliens, three metres tall, with triangular, yellow eyes and pointed ears. Zanfretta told his shocking story under hypnosis, after suffering terrible nightmares.

In-Flight Entertainment

Terrified Mario Restier was abducted by aliens from Orion and taken aboard their ship. There he was submerged up to his nose in thick, glutinous liquid. The aliens were very friendly and told him that this was necessary for his safety and nourishment. Perhaps this form of in-flight catering is something airlines might like to consider?

Beam Me Up!

Travis Walton was working in a forest in Arizona, USA in 1975. He was driving home after work with his workmates when they all saw a large, glowing object hovering over the trees at the side of the road. Travis jumped from the truck and ran towards the UFO while the other men ran off in panic. Travis later claimed that he was abducted by aliens, small, chalk-white creatures with huge eyes who examined him medically and then let him go.

Travis Walton was missing for five days and local police suspected his workmates of murder. The incident was very nearly a travesty of justice.

Bizarre

Aliens have been given their own landing strip in the Nevada Desert, USA. Route 375 is now known as the Extraterrestrial Highway and vertical road signs have been erected so that alien drivers don't get lost as they land their spaceships.

ABDUCTED!

A Bad Trip

Late one night in Haiti in the 1940s, a witch doctor was on his way home from visiting a patient when he was abducted by aliens. He reported that they drove him around town all night and that they were very ugly.

Tongue in Cheek

Betty Andreasson was abducted by aliens in 1950. They put her on a bed of jelly-like material and inserted a device in her mouth to hold her tongue in place during the rapid acceleration of the UFO. She was gob-smacked by the experience.

Route Diversion

Trucker, Harry Turner, and his lorry were abducted by an alien in August 1979. The alien was called Alpha La ZooLou and he took Harry to his home planet which had dome-covered cities. Harry Turner is probably the only lorry driver in the world who fell off the back of his own lorry.

ANCIENT ALIEN JOKE
What kind of coat does an alien wear on a rainy day?

A wet one.

What's an astronaut's favourite meal?
Launch!

Animal Abductions

I'm really a space hero

What's big and ugly and wears sunglasses? An alien on holiday

Aliens seem fascinated by animals and there have been many reported incidents Many dogs go missing every year Have you a Space Rover in your hous

Is Your Dog a Space Hero?

Does your dog have a secret life? Has he saved the universe? Does he travel though time and space and still get home for his tin of 'Chunkie'? Signs to look out for:

• Does he sleep a lot during the day?
• Does he bark at something you can't see?
• Does he sometimes desperately need to go out?
• Does he watch sci-fi movies on television like 'E.T.' or 'The Beast with a Million Eyes'?

COSMIC CHUCKLES Did you hear about the alien with five legs? His trousers fit him like a glove.

Look out Topo!

Topo Gets Topped!

Topo, the guard dog on a farm in Uruguay, suffered a nasty shock when he rushed to protect his owner from a UFO which descended on the farm. The UFO shot beams of white lightning at Topo and the rancher, then vanished. The farmer was unwell for many days but poor Topo was found dead at the very spot where he had bravely fought the alien craft. An autopsy revealed that the dog had been 'cooked' from within by a powerful electro-magnetic force. Poor Topo had been micro-waved!

K-9 Napping in New Jersey

John Trasco saw a UFO near his barn when he went to feed his dog. A metre high humanoid, looking like a leprechaun, in a green shirt and hat, approached him and said: "We come in peace. We don't want trouble. We just want your dog." Trasco told them to get lost and the aliens returned to their UFO. "They weren't gonna take ma dawg," barked Trasco.

What a Frame-Up

Four young poachers in Cheshire, England in 1978 had a searing experience when they saw two aliens place a frame around a cow and take measurements. They ran off but felt a strong tugging sensation pulling them back. One of the boys had a burning in his pants and was red and sore for days afterwards.

This is Unherd Of!

Cowboy, Larry Cardea, heard a weird humming noise and found a herd of cows being pulled through the trees by a 'strange beam'. The cowboy opened fire at the beam which then disappeared. But already one cow had completely disappeared and an udder was badly hurt.

Alien Blood Bank Collector

Farmer Lonnie Duggan in Idaho, USA surprised a furry alien who was taking blood from his horse. "I thought he was a real clot," said Lonnie. "He made my blood boil."

Close Encounters

SILLY SNIGGER
What do you call an alien who plops through your letter box
~ Bill.

????

Greetings Buck...Do not be alarmed.

Starkers!

Buck Nelson, a farmer from Missouri, USA was surprised one day in 1955 when a flying saucer landed on his farm and spacemen from Venus strolled into his house. Buck informed the UFO investigators that the aliens were 'buck-naked but friendly'.

What's big and ugly with red spots?
An alien with measles.

Bye-bye Buck

Buck continued his friendship with the Venusian aliens and made many space trips with them. From one of his visits he returned with a hairless dog. Not everyone believed Buck's stories and he was dogged by ridicule for many years.

1ST ALIEN: I flew to Mars last year.
2ND ALIEN: So did I.
1ST ALIEN: Doesn't it make your arms ache?

OUCH!

Short-Shooters

In Brazil in 1969, Antonio da Silva went fishing and became a big catch himself. Hearing strange voices, he found himself surrounded by very aggressive humanoids, wearing helmets. They were very small and hairy with long beards, bushy eyebrows and no teeth. Shooting da Silva in the legs, they burnt his jeans. He was then taken on board their spacecraft. Things looked bad for da Silva until the appearance of a tall thin alien who returned him to earth.

Josef Wanderka was riding his motorcycle near Vienna in 1955 when he saw a flying saucer land and a ramp lowered. Herr Wanderka wondered what was inside and without hesitation, he rode his bike up the ramp and into the ship. Once on board, he met aliens and found that they spoke perfect German. Herr Wanderka described the experience as wunderbar!

THEY CAME FROM OUTER SPACE!

Out of His Tree

Donald Schrum will never forget the day he went hunting in 1964 in California, USA. He became separated from his friends and as it grew dark, decided to spend the night in a tree to keep safe from predators. During the night he saw a very bright light and shortly afterwards two humanoids and a robot approached his tree. They started shaking the tree, trying to dislodge Schrum. At one point the robot belched out white vapour which made the hunter feel very sick. He fired an arrow at the robot, there was a flash and the robot recoiled. Schrum then fired more arrows at the aliens and they retreated. But yet another robot arrived and it too belched foul vapour at Schrum which knocked him unconscious. He recovered to find the aliens trying to climb the tree but he managed to fight them off. It was a very long night for Schrum but eventually the aliens returned to their ship and he was left to tell his story.

What does an alien travelling through space do when he gets dirty? He takes a meteor shower.

A Doorway in Time?

Are we being visited by visitors from another time dimension? Are there doorways in time that they can enter and travel as they wish? In 1973 an Australian couple were driving along the Eyre Highway when they saw a large orange rectangle beside the road. A very large humanoid was silhouetted against it. It looked like a huge doorway in space, they reported.

Peeping 'Mothman'

A courting couple in Kent, England were disturbed to find a seven foot 'Mothman' alien with glowing eyes peering through the back window of their car. It moth have been a horrible experience – for someone.

Tin Man in Japan

Hideichi Amano had a close encounter of the nose kind when he was accosted by a huge metal man who pressed his metal nose against Amano's forehead, possibly in an attempt to communicate. Mr Amano was rendered speechless.

THINKING OF YOU
Many aliens communicate telepathically. You don't have to worry about what you say but just be careful what you think. Beware of teachers or parents who say, 'Take that expression off your face. I know what you are thinking.'

X-Facts

To Infinity or Bust

It has often been reported that aliens wear human clothes in order to merge more easily with the people of Earth. Peculiarly, however, they do not like wearing high-heeled shoes or bras.

It...Won't Wash

Various contactees have reported that aliens rarely, if ever, wash their hands. Bear this in mind when first greeting aliens.

Ooo! Ah! I hate this bra!

Let's shake on it Earthling

I feel a heel

YESSSS!

SSSSEY!

Virtual reality

Actual reality

Is Seeing Believing?

There are frequent reports of aliens living on Earth disguised as human beings. It is thought that aliens use a cloaking device to distort their alien shape into that of an earthling. Possibly someone you know is an alien disguised as a human. Could some of your teachers be aliens?

Study them carefully for alien characteristics.

Do they glow slightly in the dark – try switching off the lights to see.

Do they ever change colour and scream incoherently?

Do they emit strange hissings, beepings or popping sounds when they think no one is listening?

Do they know what you are thinking before you say it?

Green Tentacled

Do you have an alien neighbour?
Does he wander around the garden late
at night looking at his hollyhocks?
Does he grow things in a little glass house?
Does he ever say
"It's going to rain."
And it does!

Interplanetary Pal

Could your best friend be an alien?
Is he ever weird? Can he wiggle his ears?
Does he ever drool or spit?
Does he ever make horrible sulphurous smells?
Is he ever just not all there?

The strangest possibility of all, of course, is that
YOUR MUM could be an alien.
— Do her eyes grow big and staring when she is mad? with you?
— Aliens rarely, if ever, sleep. Is your Mum awake
when you go to bed and awake when you get up in the morning?
— Aliens are very tidy. Is your Mum always telling
you to clean up your room?
— Aliens are telepathic. Does your Mum know when
you are telling fibs?
— And if you discover that your Mum is an alien
this can only mean one thing... and that is...
and that is... that...

... you are an Alien too!!

Earth is only one of the many, many
planets in our galaxy. There are
millions of other galaxies beyond our own
It is therefore extremely unlikely
that we are the only life-form
within the Universe...

... keep watching the skies!